THE ANCIENT ONE

Two anxious yellow eyes searched back and

schools of fish near the shore, and no need to
venture any farther than the mouth of the caves.
But even as it remembered, its empty stomach
yearned to be satisfied.

Wait. There was something. A tiny ratlike
creature dangled in the water just above it.

The Ancient One rose to the top.

OTHER YEARLING BOOKS YOU WILL ENJOY:

YEARLING BOOKS are designed especially to entertain and enlighten young people. Patricia Reilly Giff, consultant to this series, received her bachelor's degree from Marymount College and a master's degree in history from St. John's University. She holds a Professional Diploma in Reading and a Doctorate of Humane Letters from Hofstra University. She was a teacher and reading consultant for many years, and is the author of numerous books for young readers.

GARY PAULSEN

THE CREATURE
OF
BLACK WATER LAKE

A YEARLING BOOK

Published by
Bantam Doubleday Dell Books for Young Readers
a division of
Bantam Doubleday Dell Publishing Group, Inc.
1540 Broadway
New York, New York 10036

ISBN: 0-440-41211-0

Series design: Barbara Berger

Interior illustration by Michael David Biegel

Printed in the United States of America

July 1997

OPM 10 9 8 7 6 5 4 3 2 1

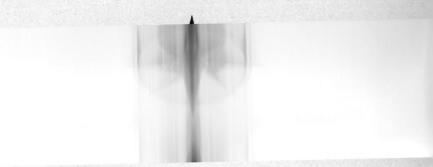

...sailing the Pacific Ocean, I've experienced some of this adventure myself. I try to capture this spirit in my stories, and each time I sit down to write, that challenge is a bit of an adventure in itself.

You're all a part of this adventure as well. Over the years I've had the privilege of talking with many of you in schools, and this book is the result of hearing firsthand what you want to read about most—power-packed adventure and excitement.

You asked for it—so hang on tight while we jump into another thrilling story in my World of Adventure.

Gary Paulsen

Two glowing yellow eyes stared up toward the light that filtered down through the darkness. They were unblinking, waiting patiently for the slightest disturbance in the water. The Ancient One didn't like coming this close to the surface but a fierce, gnawing hunger was driving it. There were hardly any large fish left on the bottom near the caves, and it had been almost five days since the Ancient One had eaten.

The smooth water suddenly rocked with movement. Something large with four thrashing limbs, odd rubbery flippers, and a hard metal can on its back approached. The Ancient One had only seen this type of fish a few times over the years. But it remembered how they tasted and how good it felt to be full and satisfied.

The Ancient One moved carefully upward.

"It's nice here, don't you think, Ryan?" The pretty blond woman's tired blue eyes traveled from the road to the thin, dark-haired boy sitting in the passenger seat beside her.

Thirteen-year-old Ryan Swanner looked out the window. The Colorado mountains were okay, but they weren't anything like the ones back home. Ryan had grown up in Louisiana, fishing on the swamps and bayous, and it had been hard to say goodbye to his friends there. But his mom was so excited about her new job that he didn't have the heart to spoil things for her. So he'd kept his feelings to himself.

She was now the new manager of a restaurant called The Cove, which catered to tourists at the Black Water Lake Resort. It was a big break for her. Back home she had waitressed at truck stops and coffee shops. This job meant a lot more money.

Ryan collected his thoughts and turned back toward his mom. "Uh, yeah. Real nice. Lots of . . . trees and stuff. It'll be great."

The old car rumbled down the narrow gravel road and turned off onto a deeply rutted dirt lane. They stopped in front of a log cabin that was almost completely covered with vines.

"This is it, Ryan. What do you think?"

Ryan opened the car door and stepped out. In ways the scenery reminded him of the thick green foliage that had surrounded their house back home. But there was something different about the quiet and the crispness of the air here. He stepped up onto the wooden porch and was about to reach for the doorknob when a large woman wearing baggy jeans and a red flannel shirt stepped out of the cabin, shaking a dusty rug in his face.

"Oh my!" She drew back and tried to wave

Mrs. Brown. I'm Cynthia Swanner and this is my son, Ryan."

The woman surveyed him. "Rita has been looking forward to meeting you. Annie was hoping for a girl. But she's only four so I'm sure she'll make do." Mrs. Brown smiled. "I'll get out of your way now and let the two of you unpack and get settled. If you need anything, my house is the yellow one just over the hill behind you." She gave a friendly wave and marched off into the woods.

They watched her leave and then Ryan's mom pushed the cabin door open. "Mrs. Brown told me we're not far from the lodge, and Black Water Lake is within walking distance."

Water. That was one thing Ryan knew something about. Maybe it wouldn't be so awful here after all.

The inside of the cabin was small but cozy. Cynthia Swanner stopped to smell the wildflowers that stood in a vase on the kitchen table. "It already feels like home."

Ryan hadn't seen his mom this happy in years—not since before the car accident that had taken his dad's life. "I think it's gonna be just fine, Mom. Just fine."

Ryan moved the branch of a pine tree and there it was—the lake. The water lay flat and shiny like a big black slab of onyx. This was the Black Water Lake the resort was named for. It was a large, kidney-shaped body of water as dark as its name. This end of the lake was some distance from the lodge, which was hidden from sight by hills and trees.

"Couldn't get much better." Ryan stepped out onto the sandy shore and skipped a rock across the lake's smooth surface.

He dipped his hand in the water and found

it a little colder than he'd expected. Still, a quick swim would be fun. He sat down and began pulling off his tennis shoes.

"Wouldn't do that if I were you."

Ryan spun around. Standing behind him was a tall redheaded girl with her arms folded.

"H-Hi," Ryan began. "I was just—"

The girl pointed to a sign on the shore. "Can't you read?"

Ryan hadn't noticed the small weather-beaten sign:

CLOSED TO ALL SWIMMING AND DIVING

UNTIL FURTHER NOTICE.

"I guess I missed that."

The girl sat down beside Ryan in the dirt. "I'm Rita Brown. You're living in our grandpa's old cabin."

Ryan relaxed and slipped his shoes back on. "I'm Ryan Swanner. I was just gonna see what the water was like. Do you swim?"

"Used to," Rita said, "until that diver got himself drowned last week. They're still look-ing for his body. Ma says the owners of the

8

lodge won't allow any swimming till they find him. She doesn't believe there's a monster,

"Naw. It's a story the locals made up years ago to draw tourists." Rita tossed a stick into the water. "Some places have ghosts. Black Water has a monster."

Ryan studied the lake with a frown. "If you don't go out in the water, what do you do around here for fun?"

Rita jumped up. "Who says I don't go out there? Come with me."

Ryan followed Rita down the shore to a shallow inlet. Resting in a cluster of weeds was a beat-up rectangular wooden raft with a long rope anchoring it to a tree.

"We need to do some work on it before we can take it out again," Rita said. "It leaks 'cause some of the boards are broken and loose. But when it works, the fishing's better out from shore a ways."

"Fishing?" Ryan raised one eyebrow. "What do you catch?"

"Everything. One time I caught a catfish that was so big, Ma had a hard time cooking it. Course that was a year or so ago. The big ones seem to have just about disappeared."

Behind them something slapped the top of the lake hard. The sound echoed across the water.

"What was that?" Ryan turned and pointed to the disappearing ripples.

"It was probably one of those big catfish I was talking about." Rita moved to the edge of the water. "We'll catch him just as soon as we get this raft in shape."

"Whatever it was, it sure left some big ripples in the water," Ryan said. "They're as big around as your grandfather's cabin."

Rita smiled at him. "Are you *scared*?" she asked teasingly.

Ryan looked her in the eye. "No way."

Rita cocked her head. "Well, don't let the ghost stories get to you. Tell you what. If you help me work on the raft, we'll go out fishing on it. What do you say?"

"Let's get started."

Two anxious yellow eyes searched back and forth continuously. The Ancient One was hungry all the time now. The food supply was dwindling and anything large or small that dared disturb the calm waters was considered a meal.

It remembered a time when there was no need to hunt, no need to gobble down the small schools of fish near the shore, and no need to venture any farther than the mouth of the caves. But even as it remembered, its empty stomach yearned to be satisfied.

Wait. There was something. A tiny ratlike creature dangled in the water just above it.

The Ancient One rose to the top.

CHAPTER 3

"Remember to come down to the lodge for lunch. It's only about a thirty-minute walk from here to the upper end of the lake. I'd like to show you off to the staff." Ryan's mother started the engine of the old car and waved as she pulled out of the drive.

Ryan waved back and then raced around the cabin and up the hill. On the other side of the hill was the large two-story yellow house where the Browns lived.

He trotted down the path and hopped up

onto the porch. There was no doorbell so he knocked lightly and waited.

[illegible text obscured]

Oh, hi, Ryan. Ready to work.

"What exactly are you two going to do to-day?" Mrs. Brown put her hand on her daughter's shoulder.

Ryan began, "We're going down to the lake and fix—"

"Fish," Rita interrupted. "We're just going to fish and maybe do some other stuff."

"Just make sure the *other* stuff doesn't include swimming," Mrs. Brown said. "I know there's no monster in that lake, but I don't want you going back in until they find that diver."

"Right, Ma. Don't worry about a thing." Rita stepped out onto the porch and pulled the door shut. She motioned for Ryan to follow her around the back of the house.

13

"Whew. That was close." Rita waited for Ryan to catch up. "I forgot to mention that Ma doesn't know anything about the raft. I figured we were really doing her a favor by not telling her. You know, one less thing to worry about."

"Got it." Ryan followed Rita to an old shed behind the house.

Rita rummaged around on the dusty shelves until she found some rope, a couple of old oars, a can of black pitch, and several long flat boards. She handed Ryan some of the supplies and led the way down the path to the lake.

The raft was still in the weeds where they'd left it the day before. Together they hauled it up onto the shore.

"See, the middle boards are cracked and some of the rope is coming loose on that end." Rita pointed to the right side. "I figure we'll replace the boards, make sure it's all good and tight, then use some of this pitch to coat the bottom. She'll be unsinkable."

Ryan knelt and began working the cracked boards loose. Rita took out her pocketknife and cut a piece off the long coil of rope.

14

When the first board was out, Rita handed
Ryan a replacement and helped him secure it

on the bottom of the raft and trying to
smooth it across the boards.

The bushes near the path to the Browns'
house rustled and Annie stepped out. She
walked up to the raft and looked it over. "You
shouldn't go out on the water. The *thing* will
get you."

Rita was stooped over holding the pitch
brush. She wiped the sweat off her forehead.
"Go away, Annie. We're busy here."

Annie stared out into the lake. "I've seen it.
It ate my dog."

"That's nice. Now go play."

"Ma has lunch ready. She says you guys
better hurry or she'll feed it to the pigs." Annie turned and marched back into the trees.

Ryan watched her go. "What does she
mean—she's seen it?"

"Don't pay any attention to Annie. She's always saying stuff like that. One time she came down here by herself looking for her puppy. She never found it. So now she tells everybody that the monster jumped out of the water and dragged her dog in." Rita shook her head and sighed. "Kids. So, do you want to come over for lunch?"

Ryan looked at his watch. "I can't. My mom's expecting me. How do I get to the lodge from here?"

"That way." Rita pointed down the shore. "Just follow the lake. You can't get lost. Hey, if you're not doing anything, come over later. We'll get this finished up so we can take it out first thing tomorrow."

"Okay—I'll be back," Ryan said, doing his best Schwarzenegger imitation.

Rita laughed and waved. "See ya, Arnold."

 Ryan passed the dock and climbed the wooden steps to the restaurant. The Cove was made of hand-hewn logs and stone, like a giant cabin. It stood on the edge of the lake and the dark water reflected off the large plate glass windows in front.

Several guests were eating as Ryan made his way across the dining room. His mother was standing by a rock fireplace talking to one of the waiters when she noticed him.

"Hi, kiddo. Nice of you to make it." She

looked down at the toe of his shoe, which was covered with tar. "What in the world . . . ?"

"It's tar. Rita Brown was working on a project and I was helping her. I guess I kinda made a mess. I'll see if I can get it off later."

"Try paint thinner. And if that doesn't work maybe kerosene." A sandy-haired waiter stuck out his hand. "I'm Larry Carlson."

"Larry is a college student," Mrs. Swanner explained. "He works here part-time in the summer."

Ryan shook Larry's hand. "I didn't know there was a college around here."

The young man smiled. "There isn't. I sort of migrate here from California every year. Some of the classes you have to take for marine biology can fry your brain if you're not careful. I come down here to unwind more than anything else."

"Larry, why don't you find Ryan a nice out-of-the-way table, and I'll go talk the cook into making him something to eat."

"I'm in kind of a hurry, Mom. Rita and I are trying to get an old raft in shape to take fishing tomorrow."

"Sounds like fun, but you have to eat. Hang

18

on—I'll wrap something up for you." She headed for the kitchen.

on. But I think it's the plant life. I've been doing some tests in different areas on the bottom—"

"You've been to the bottom?" Ryan couldn't believe it. "Didn't you hear about that other diver?"

"Oh, sure. But accidents happen. To tell you the truth, I don't really have much faith in the monster legend. It's a nice story, but not too many prehistoric creatures are still alive after two hundred and fifty million years. And if they were, I doubt they'd be living at the bottom of a lake."

"Really? Well, I guess worrying about a monster is the last way I wanted to spend my summer," Ryan said.

"Let me know if you catch anything tomorrow." Larry took out his order pad. "I guess I

19

better get back to work before your mom fires me. It was nice meeting you, Ryan."

"You too."

"Here you go." Ryan's mother came out of the kitchen with a brown bag. "Well, what do you think of the restaurant?"

"It's great! Larry seems real nice, too."

"He is. In fact, the whole staff is. And I'm glad things are working out for you, too. Bring Rita down sometime and have lunch on me."

As Ryan left the restaurant, he thought over what Larry had told him. Larry sure seemed to know what he was talking about.

But what kind of lake is completely fishless? thought Ryan.

The black water was murky. Billowy clouds of soil hung in the water because of the recent disturbance in the area.

The cold eyes below the surface were used to these conditions. The Ancient One could still easily spot its prey hanging from the tree branch overhead. The prey was making loud noises and seemed to be unaware of the Ancient One's presence.

Quietly it waited. Hoping. Perhaps the animal would slip, or the tree limb would break. The expectation made the Ancient One quiver in anticipation. Juices released from somewhere deep inside its body made their way to its mouth.

A noise distracted it. Another, smaller animal was thrashing about in the water a few yards away. The long neck of the Ancient One flexed and its large head snaked forward. Curved teeth fastened like a vise and it was over. The animal struggled for less than a second; then it was swiftly and effortlessly dragged to the bottom.

Ryan was trying to decide whether he should start without Rita. The pitch was dry and the only thing left to do was to put the raft on the water and see if it would float.

It was early. The sun was barely up. Ryan checked his bait again and put his fishing gear next to a tree. He spotted a huge pine with branches that leaned out several feet over the water.

The tree was easy to climb. He swung out onto one of the lower branches and looked down into the water. It was cloudy and for some reason an odd shiver ran through him. He started to climb back.

"I used to have a rope on that one!" Rita yelled from the bushes, nearly making Ryan fall. "But the lake patrol made me take it down."

Ryan spotted his friend on the shore. "I can see why. It would be perfect for swinging out into the water." He pulled himself up on top of the branch. "I used to have one a lot like it back home."

In a nearby tree Ryan saw a fat squirrel run out to the edge of a branch. The branch was low on the tree and reached out over the lake. The squirrel looked as though it was about to jump into the lake, using the branch as a diving board.

Ryan smiled at the funny creature and started to climb down. Suddenly there was a splash, and Ryan turned just in time to see the squirrel disappear into the water.

A larger than normal wave hit the shore and then rolled back.

"What the—?" Ryan watched the place where the squirrel had gone down, but it

never surfaced. "That was weird. Almost like
something reached up and got it."

Ryan opened his bait box. "We didn't really
have a lot to choose from. I brought cheese,
corn, and some worms. What do they bite
around here?"

"To tell you the truth, I haven't caught
much of anything in a long time. But back
when they were biting, I did my best work
with goldfish." She patted a metal can. "I've
got plenty for both of us."

"Great. Let's get out there." Ryan untied the
rope from the tree and helped Rita carry the
raft to the water. They flipped it over and set
it down gently.

"I'll go first," Rita said. "You can hand me
the oars and the fishing gear." She stepped
onto the raft and waited for Ryan to collect
everything.

They each took an oar and pushed off. The raft slowly floated away from shore.

"How far out do we go?" Ryan asked.

"It won't do any good to go too far out. This ought to about do it." Rita pulled her oar out of the water and grabbed her fishing pole. "Make sure you're using a pretty strong line. It doesn't happen very often, but when one of those big catfish gets on, it really gives you a time."

Ryan checked his line and hooks and reached for some bait. He was about to cast when something moved in the water below. He blinked and looked again. There it was, inches below the surface—a giant head with sinister yellow eyes staring back at him.

"It's true!" Ryan shouted. He threw his pole down on the raft and grabbed an oar. "Row, Rita! There's something down there."

Rita froze. Before them, something huge and snakelike slithered through the water near the raft and disappeared. Then a massive flat black flipper slapped the surface of the water, leaving enormous ripples like the ones they'd seen the day before.

The wake sent a wave of water crashing

over the top of the raft and tossed it around like a tiny paper boat. It was all they could do to keep from falling into the lake.

They sat for several minutes, not saying a word, just shaking and breathing hard and staring at the water. Finally Rita spoke in a trembling voice. "It was bigger than a house. Did you see it?"

Ryan nodded dully. "I saw it. I looked it right in the eyes. They were round and yellow. I've never seen anything so terrible in all my life. It was like looking at . . . death."

CHAPTER 6

"Larry, can I talk to you a minute?" Ryan pulled the waiter to the nearest vacant table in the restaurant. "I need your help."

"Can it wait until I deliver this food to those people over there? They look like good tippers."

"Sorry. Sure, I'll just sit here till you're through."

After a minute Larry returned with a friendly smile. He settled into an empty chair at Ryan's table. "So what's going on?"

Ryan swallowed. "I've seen it."

"It?"

"The monster."

Larry cocked his head. "What exactly did

water. It had a flipper on the end of its head was huge, with big yellow eyes on either side."

Larry ran his hand through his hair. "How many of you saw it?"

"Two of us. We saw it real clear."

Larry tapped the table, thinking. "Are you sure your friend wasn't just pulling a good joke on you? You *are* the new kid in town. Maybe it was some kind of initiation prank."

"It wasn't a joke. Here." Ryan took the pen from Larry's order pad and drew on a napkin. "This is what I saw."

"That's not a lot to go on, Ryan," Larry said, studying the drawing.

"It is if you put it together with what Rita says other people have seen. The monster really is there."

"Okay. Suppose I buy your story. What do you want me to do?"

"You said you were a marine biologist. You probably know some scientists or professor types who would be interested in this thing. Maybe we could catch it or something."

"I said I was studying to *become* a marine biologist." Larry sighed. "Tell you what. I do have one professor who might be interested. He has this theory about ancient sea creatures being trapped inland in ponds and lakes when the glaciers receded. I've always thought he was sort of eccentric but I'll give him a call and see what he says. In the meantime, you and your friend stay out of the water and keep an eye on the place you saw the monster come up—just in case it was your imagination. Sometimes the mind has a way of playing tricks on you."

"Thanks, Larry. But the monster's no trick. It's as real as me and you."

There were strange vibrations in the water. Something large had entered the lake. The Ancient One quickly swallowed the warm furry creature it had intended to drag away to its lair and rose to the top to investigate.

It made a pass underneath the intruder, which was wide and flat and big enough to block out the sunlight. But the intruder didn't smell like food—or did it?

Finally the Ancient One decided this thing was no different than the large floating objects at the other end of the lake. Only it didn't churn up the water and leave dark smelly clouds in the air. The Ancient One angrily sped past the thing that was not food, slapping the surface with its tail fin to show its frustration.

Ryan walked down the row of one-room cabins that had been built to house The Cove's summer employees. He spotted number nine and knocked on the door.

"Come in. I'm on the phone."

He opened the door and Larry motioned for him to enter. Ryan looked for a place to sit down. There was a single unmade bed pushed up against the front wall, a small round table covered with books, and two chairs.

The cover of a thick book on the table caught Ryan's eye. *Sightings of the Loch Ness*

Monster. He sat down and saw several newspaper clippings. One headline read, "Giant Leatherback Turtle Found in Bottomless Pond." Another said, "Largest Eel in History of North America Found Washed up on Shore."

Larry hung up the phone and rubbed his hands together. "Dr. Townsend is sending us some equipment. He's the professor I told you about. He's willing to go out on a limb, hoping it will prove some of his theories."

"What's all this?" Ryan picked up one of the clippings. "I thought you said you didn't believe in the monster."

"I said I didn't have a lot of faith in it," Larry said sheepishly. "But I figured it couldn't hurt to stay on top of what other people have seen just in case."

"When is the stuff supposed to get here?"

"End of the week. Which means we have a lot of work to do between now and then. Your mom could only give me a few days off. We have to get my boat ready and do as many interviews as possible."

"Interviews?"

"Of people who claim to have seen the

monster. You know the old-timers around here all have stories to tell. Our job will be to

Larry handed Ryan

"How are you at hanging on?"

"Good—I think."

Larry grabbed a tape recorder off a shelf over his bed. "Then let's go. We've got a lot of ground to cover and a short time to do it in."

CHAPTER 8

"That was a big waste of time." Ryan stuffed the tape recorder into the motorcycle's saddlebag. "Mr. Potter forgot what he was talking about in the middle of his story and the nurse had to wheel him off to bed because he fell asleep."

"True," Larry admitted. "But the telephone interview with the wife of that diver who went down last week was interesting. She said he made two dives that day. On the first one he thought he'd discovered where something extremely large had made its bed in one of the caves on the bottom. After he went back the second time, no one ever saw him

from our list and go visit the Bro...

"Now you're talking." Ryan waited for Larry to get on and then hopped on the back of the cycle. Larry popped the clutch and they flew down the road toward the other side of the lake.

Rita and her mom were in the front yard pulling weeds. When the motorcycle roared into the driveway Rita trotted over.

"This is Larry Carlson," Ryan said. "He's the guy I told you was gonna help us find the monster. He wants to ask you some questions about what you saw."

"Hi, Larry," Rita said. Then she ran into the house, calling over her shoulder, "Hang on a minute."

Mrs. Brown came over to them. "Nice to

37

meet you, Mr. Carlson. Now, what's this I hear about you helping these kids look for a lake monster?"

Larry sat on the edge of the porch and took out his tape recorder. "Have you ever seen the lake monster, Mrs. Brown?"

"Heavens no. My father claimed he saw it, though. He used to fish for catfish in the lake until the day he thought he saw the monster. After that he never took his boat out on the water again. Never let us go out there either. But I think he was seeing things. You know—hallucinations."

Rita came back carrying a tattered book held together with a rubber band. "Here's my granddad's diary. The places where he talks about the monster are marked."

Larry snapped off the rubber band and opened the yellowed pages of the diary to a bookmark. He read aloud:

"I had heard the stories but always thought that was exactly what they were, stories. Now I know different. As usual I was out on the lake at daybreak fishing. It

was a slow morning but finally I hooked something. The big catfish are fighters

and get out of there, when all of a
a gigantic creature cleared the water,
grabbed my cat and took off. The rod was
jerked out of my hands and I just stood
there watching the place where I saw the
thing go down.

"Now, back at my cabin, as I try to de-
scribe what I saw, all I can say is it had
the body of a dinosaur. Its head was like a
giant fish, maybe a whale or a shark. But
its eyes are the thing I remember most.
They were evil-looking. I never want to
look in them again."

Larry closed the book. "This is great. Thank you, Rita. I'm sure your grandfather's observations will be very helpful."

"You still want to interview me, don't you?" Rita asked.

"You bet." Larry turned on the tape recorder. "For the record, state your name and age and then in your own words tell us what happened and what you saw."

 The boat's motor sputtered and then roared to life. Larry shifted into reverse and slowly backed away from the dock. "Here, Rita, take over while I check the computer screen." He stood and waited for her to move up. "Are you both sure it's all right for you to be out here?"

Rita slid into the driver's seat, pushed the throttle forward, and expertly steered the boat toward the middle of Black Water Lake.

Ryan cleared his throat. "Uh, Rita and I are allowed to come as long as we . . . uh . . ."

"As long as we're with you." Rita smiled

innocently up at Larry. "Our parents trust you."

Ryan stepped back to give Larry room to work. The biology student flipped a switch, which caused an immediate low steady beeping. "Sonar," he explained. He pointed at the screen. "This shows the topography on the bottom of the lake and registers the depth."

Ryan could see the outlines of valleys, hills, and gulleys underwater. He watched Larry turn on the tracking device. "What are you going to do with the monster once we find it?"

"Try to capture it, of course, before the big shots at the university have a chance. That's what that tranquilizer gun and the weighted net are for." He pointed at the box in the center of the boat. "If we can get the net over it, it'll wear itself out trying to get loose. Then we'll use the boat to drag it back to the corral we built at the shallow end of the lake. Hopefully the log poles and rails we used are strong enough to hold it."

"Then what?"

"After that, it's hard to say. Once we have the creature contained, it will be studied, perhaps taken to an aquatic zoo." Larry winked

~~Ryan.~~ "But first we have to find it."

were almost as clear on the monitor as if they
were on dry land.

Larry adjusted the volume on the sonar.
Nothing happened. "The creature's not in
these caves or the sonar would register its
movement. But I still want to go down and
have a look. This area would be the perfect
place for it to hide in." He moved to the porta-
ble shark cage they had attached to the boat
with a series of pulleys and a crank to make it
easier to raise and lower. The cage was designed to protect shark photographers. The
bars were just a few inches apart and made of
hardened steel.

Larry checked his air tank and slid into the
harness. For added protection he loaded an
underwater speargun. "Hand me the video
camera."

43

Ryan helped Larry wrap the camera cord around his wrist. "Be careful down there."

"I will. You guys just keep an eye on the monitor and you'll be able to see everything I'm doing." Larry stepped into the cage. "I'm ready. Lower away."

Rita helped Ryan turn the crank that plunged the cage into the chilly water. They took turns until the cable went limp and the cage came to a stop on the bottom.

On the screen they could see the rough shape of Larry and the outline of the cage near the opening of the largest cave. Larry turned on the light mounted on top of the camera and began taping.

There were no fish in the area, so the only movement on the screen was Larry. The minutes ticked by and nothing disturbed the sonar.

Ryan watched as Larry unhooked the cage door and stepped out.

Rita's jaw went slack. "I can't believe this. He's going inside the cave."

Ryan's eyes widened. He swallowed and reached for the spare tank of air, quickly wiggling into the harness.

Rita grabbed his arm. "Are you crazy? What do you think you're doing?"

THE ANCIENT ONE

Hunting was poor. The Ancient One had been away from its lair for hours and had nothing to show for its time except the already forgotten taste of a few small fish.

That would have to do. The water up here was too warm and made it uneasy.

Down in the caves it would sleep—until the hunger drove it to the top.

The Ancient One headed back.

Larry pointed toward the surface and motioned angrily for Ryan to go back up.

Ryan shook his head, gesturing for both of them to enter the shark cage.

Larry hesitated and then turned into the cave.

Ryan had no choice but to follow. The cave was large and dark. The only light came from the video camera, and it was just a narrow beam.

At the back of the cave, tunnels led in several directions. Larry headed toward the first one. Ryan tapped his shoulder. The opening was only a few feet wide. From what he'd seen, the monster wouldn't be able to fit its head through, much less its giant body.

Ryan motioned toward the other side. Larry swung the light around, nodded, and swam to a larger tunnel. A few feet inside, the tunnel made a sharp turn and then opened into a large round cavity that dead-ended into solid rock.

Larry pointed the light at the floor. A mangled diving tank lay on a pile of other strange objects that included tin cans, fishing poles . . . and bones.

A lump of fear rose in Ryan's throat. It was true! The monster had eaten that diver. It would eat them too if it caught them in its den.

Larry turned and pointed the light back toward the tunnel. Ryan nodded and wasted no time following him out of the cave.

He was glad to see the shark cage, and he felt even better when they were inside and it jerked upward as Rita cranked it to the surface.

"So?" Rita helped Ryan out of the tank harness. "What did you find down there?"

"It lives there, Rita!" Ryan exclaimed. "We found its den."

"Wow!" Rita leaned against the steering wheel. "You guys are lucky it didn't get you. What do we do now?"

Larry made some quick notes in a logbook. "There are very few fish of any size left in the lake. The creature probably would never leave the caves except for the fact that food is getting harder and harder for it to find."

"Okay, so the thing is out looking for food."

Rita scratched her head. "Then how are we supposed to find it?"

"I don't think the creature likes going up to the warmer layers of water. It probably stays as close to the caves as possible."

"So all we have to do is wait around until it comes home." Ryan sighed.

"Hopefully we won't have long to wait." Larry reached into a large ice chest and pulled out two good-sized fish. "Let's see if we can persuade it to come to dinner."

"I'm not so sure about this." Ryan chewed his lip. "You haven't seen the monster—it's awfully big."

"Quit worrying. By the end of the day we're going to have enough evidence to bring an army of scientists down here."

"Or die trying," Rita muttered.

Larry strapped on the camera, grabbed the fish, and stepped back into the cage. "If this works, as soon as you spot the creature, give me a few minutes to tape, then get me back up here quick so I can help with the net."

"You got it." Ryan lowered the cage, and

then he and Rita watched the screens. Larry
near the entrance of the
the two

Something very
the cage.

"There it is, Ryan!" Rita yelled. "It's taking
the bait!"

Larry dropped the dead fish on the muddy
lake bottom and began taping. The creature
bumped the cage, searching for the food. It
couldn't find the fish, so it turned around and
bumped the cage again, harder.

"We'd better bring him up, Rita!" Ryan
tried to turn the crank. "Oh no. It's stuck!"

Rita ran to help. They both pulled with all
their might, but the mechanism refused to
turn.

"The cable must be twisted." Ryan glanced
at the computer screen. The monster contin-
ued to ram the cage again and again with its
massive head.

"Why doesn't he shoot it?" Rita watched the screen nervously.

"Uh-oh." Ryan spun around. "That's why."

Lying next to the open ice chest on the deck of the boat was Larry's speargun.

"It's going to kill him." Rita pointed at the screen. The creature had the corner of the cage locked in its giant teeth and was shaking it mercilessly. The softer metal on the roof was tearing loose.

Larry flew against the side bars and crashed to the floor.

"He's not getting up, Ryan. I think he's hurt. . . . Ryan? What are you doing?"

Ryan already had the spare tank of air strapped on again. He picked up the speargun. "Keep trying to get the cage up."

Rita nodded dully and moved to the crank. Ryan slipped over the side of the boat into the black turbid water.

He stayed in the shadows and cautiously headed for the light from the video camera. The monster was so intent on Larry that it didn't notice him.

When the monster circled for another

charge, Ryan swam to the top of the cage and

was slumped in the cor-

monster.

Still moving cautiously, Ryan moved
side to inspect the cable. It had twisted inside
the pulley on the top of the cage. He braced
against the metal bars and yanked with all his
strength. The rigid cable snapped into posi-
tion.

Rita had been watching the whole thing on
the monitor and immediately started hauling
them up. At the surface Ryan jumped from the
top of the cage into the boat and helped Rita
crank it the rest of the way up.

Inside the dented cage, Larry was standing,
still holding his ribs.

"Hang on." Ryan reached for the bars to
pull him in. "We'll have you out in just a second."

The cage was tottering on the edge of the

boat when the angry monster surfaced. Ryan couldn't believe his eyes. The thing looked different out of the water, like a space creature—it was huge and ugly, and it jumped and smacked the top of the water with its tail, then plunged back down.

The boat lurched as the creature came up hard beneath it. Ryan lost his balance and fell, hitting his head on the sharp corner of the metal cage. He tumbled, half-conscious, back into the murky water.

"The speargun, Rita!" Larry called weakly. "Hurry."

Ryan felt dizzy and light-headed. Something slammed past him, flipping him over. He breathed in a mouthful of water and choked, and his eyes flew open.

A few yards in front of him was the face of the monster. Its jaws were opened wide—showing a slimy white throat and rows and rows of jagged teeth.

The creature moved in for the kill. Ryan was going to die. A second, maybe two, and he would be torn to pieces. The mouth was there, open, on him.

Suddenly the monster jerked sideways. The

head was so close to Ryan he felt the brush of

skin. A stream of dark liquid

writhed in

Chapter 12

"Are you okay?" Rita helped Ryan climb into the boat.

Ryan nodded and collapsed onto the deck. "Man . . . I thought . . . I thought I was a goner."

Larry shrugged out of his gear and crouched beside Ryan. "That was as close as I ever want to come. It took me a minute to locate you and when I did, I saw the creature, too. It was closing in. When I shot it I must have hurt it because it veered off and ran for cover in one of the caves."

Ryan tried to catch his breath. "What hap-
~~~ now?"

~~~~~~~~~~~~~~~~~~~~~~~~ said, lean-

Ryan sat up. "Are you sure ~~~~~~~~~~~
want? I'm okay. We can try again . . ."

Larry shook his head. "No. It would be sui-
cide. Thanks to you and Rita, the world will
be able to see what the creature looks like. I
think you've done enough." He looked at Rita.
"Take us home, Skipper."

Rita started the motor and slowly piloted
the boat across the water. Ryan stared over the
back of the boat at the dark water, looking for
some sign of the creature, but there was nothing. Not a ripple.

THE ANCIENT ONE

The Ancient One knew by instinct that it was dying. Something incredibly sharp had pierced the side of its neck and it was fast losing blood.

It couldn't remember how long this lake had been its home but knew it would miss the lake. A faint picture came into its brain, an almost genetic memory of other creatures somewhere, like it, in other dark caves. And then the picture was gone.

The Ancient One moved as far back in the cave as possible. The lids of its eyes closed, opened, closed, and did not open again.

GARY PAULSEN

ADVENTURE GUIDE

MYTHICAL MONSTERS

You've probably heard of Bigfoot and the Loch Ness Monster. These are creatures that people claim to have seen but whose existence has never been proved. The study of these mysterious creatures is called cryptozoology, which literally means the study of hidden animals. Cryptozoology is not a recognized branch of the science of zoology. It is a controversial field. Cryptozoologists use legends and stories of sightings to try to establish the existence of these strange creatures.

Bigfoot is probably the most famous mythic monster. Also called Sasquatch, it is thought to be a huge, hair-covered biped. A biped is an animal that walks on two feet—like a human. Some think Bigfoot descended from the extinct Gigantopithecus, the largest ape that ever lived. Bigfoot sightings occur frequently in the American North-

west. But so far, no evidence has been presented that proves that this giant creature exists.

The Loch Ness Monster, also known as Nessie,

Giant squid have been fishermen's nets but no scientist has ever observed one alive in its natural habitat. The giant squid is believed to be the largest animal in the world, growing to sixty or seventy feet long with eyes the size of dinner plates.

There are many other types of creatures—giant and mysterious cats, birds, and reptiles, for example—that cryptozoologists have investigated. Some cryptozoologists even believe that some creatures thought to be extinct may still walk the earth. Could there still be dinosaurs alive today? Is Bigfoot just a hoax? We may never know for sure.

Don't miss all the exciting action!

Red Horse ...

ple, was beheaded, and now haunts the Sacramento Mountain range, searching for his head. To Will and Sarah it's just a story—until they decide to explore a newfound mountain cave, a cave filled with dangerous treasures.

Deep underground, Will and Sarah uncover an old chest stuffed with a million dollars. But now armed bandits are after them. When they find a gold Apache statue hidden in a skull, it seems Red Horse is hunting them too. Then they lose their way, and each step they take in the damp, dark cavern could be their last.

Rodomonte's Revenge

Friends Brett Wilder and Tom Houston are video game whizzes. So when a new virtual reality arcade called Rodomonte's Revenge opens near their home, they make sure they're its first customers. The game is awesome. There are flaming fire rivers to jump, beastly buzz-bugs to fight, and ugly tunnel spiders to escape. If they're good enough they'll face

Rodomonte, an evil giant waiting to do battle within his hidden castle.

But soon after they play the game, strange things start happening to Brett and Tom. The computer is taking over their minds. Now everything that happens in the game is happening in real life. A buzz-bug could gnaw off their ears. Rodomonte could smash them to bits. Brett and Tom have no choice but to play Rodomonte's Revenge again. This time they'll be playing for their lives.

Escape from Fire Mountain

". . . please, anybody . . . fire . . . need help."

That's the urgent cry thirteen-year-old Nikki Roberts hears over the CB radio the weekend she's left alone in her family's hunting lodge. The message also says that the sender is trapped near a bend in the river. Nikki knows it's dangerous, but she has to try to help. She paddles her canoe downriver, coming closer to the thick black smoke of the forest fire with each stroke. When she reaches the bend, Nikki climbs onshore. There, covered with soot and huddled on a rock ledge, sit two small children.

Nikki struggles to get the children to safety. Flames roar around them. Trees splinter to the ground. But as Nikki tries to escape the fire, she doesn't know that two poachers are also hot on her trail. They fear that she and the children have seen too much of their illegal operation—and they'll do anything to keep the kids from making it back to the lodge alive.

The Rock Jockeys

Devil's Wall.

As the [illegible] ble upon the plane's battered shell. Inside, [illegible] items that seem to have belonged to the crew, including a diary written by the navigator. Spud later falls into a deep hole and finds something even more frightening: a human skull and bones. To find out where they might have come from, the boys read the navigator's story in the diary. It reveals a gruesome secret that heightens the dangers the mountain might hold for the Rock Jockeys.

Hook 'Em, Snotty!

Bobbie Walker loves working on her grandfather's ranch. She hates the fact that her cousin Alex is coming up from Los Angeles to visit and will probably ruin her summer. Alex can barely ride a horse and doesn't know the first thing about roping. There is no way Alex can survive a ride into the flats to round up wild cattle. But Bobbie is going to have to let her tag along anyway.

Out in the flats the weather turns bad. Even worse, Bobbie knows that she'll have to watch out for the

Bledsoe boys, two mischievous brothers who are usually up to no good. When the boys rustle the girls' cattle, Bobbie and Alex team up to teach the Bledsoes a lesson. But with the wild bull Diablo on the loose, the fun and games may soon turn deadly serious.

Danger on Midnight River

Daniel Martin doesn't want to go to Camp Eagle Nest. He wants to spend the summer as he always does: with his uncle Smitty in the Rocky Mountains. Daniel is a slow learner, but most other kids call him retarded. Daniel knows that at camp, things are only going to get worse. His nightmare comes true when he and three bullies must ride the camp van together.

On the trip to camp, Daniel is the butt of the bullies' jokes. He ignores them and concentrates on the roads outside. He thinks they may be lost. As the van crosses a wooden bridge, the planks suddenly give way. The van plunges into the raging river below. Daniel struggles to shore, but the driver and the other boys are nowhere to be found. It's freezing, and night is setting in. Daniel faces a difficult decision. He could save himself . . . or risk everything to try to rescue the others too.

The Gorgon Slayer

Eleven-year-old Warren Trumbull has a strange job. He works for Prince Charming's Damsel in Distress

Rescue Agency, saving people from hideous monsters, evil warlocks, and wicked witches. Then one day Warren gets the most dangerous assignment of

The Gorgon howls as Warren enters the dark basement to do battle. Warren lowers his eyes, raises his sword and shield, and leaps into action. But will his plan work?

Captive!

Roman Sanchez is trying hard to deal with the death of his dad—a SWAT team member gunned down in the line of duty. But Roman's nightmare is just beginning.

When masked gunmen storm into his classroom, Roman and three other boys are taken hostage. They are thrown into the back of a truck and hauled to a run-down mountain cabin, miles from anywhere. They are bound with rope and given no food. With each passing hour the kidnappers' deadly threats become even more real.

Roman knows time is running out. Now he must somehow put his dad's death behind him so that he

and the others can launch a last desperate fight for
freedom.

The Treasure of El Patrón

Tag Jones and his friend Cowboy spend their days
diving in the azure water surrounding Bermuda. It's
not just for fun—Tag knows that somewhere in the
coral reef there's a sunken ship full of treasure. His
father died in a diving accident looking for the ship,
and Tag won't give up until he finds it.

Then the ship's manifest of the Spanish galleon *El
Patrón* turns up, and Tag can barely contain his excitement. *El Patrón* sank in 1614, carrying "un-
known cargo." Tag knows that *this* is the ship his
father was looking for. And he's not the least bit
scared off by the rumors that *El Patrón* is cursed. But
when two tourists want Tag to retrieve some mysterious sunken parcels for them, Tag and Cowboy may
be in dangerous water, way over their heads!

Skydive!

Jesse Rodriguez has a pretty exciting job for a thirteen-year-old, working at a small flight and skydiving school near Seattle. Buck Sellman, the owner of
the school, lets Jesse help out around the airport and
is teaching him all about skydiving. Jesse can't wait
until he's sixteen and old enough to make his first
jump.

Then Robin Waterford walks in with her father one
day to sign up for lessons, and strange things start to

happen. Photographs that Robin takes of the airfield mysteriously disappear from her locker. And Robin and Jesse discover that someone at the airfield is in-

Chosen One,

The ancient palace lies in the Valley of Zon. It is imperative that you come immediately. You are my last hope. Look for the secret path. The stars will lead the way.

Take care. The eyes of Mogg are everywhere.

As if school bullies weren't enough of a problem, now Chris Masters has a computer game pushing him around! Ever since The Seventh Crystal arrived anonymously in the mail one day, Chris has been obsessed with it—it's the most challenging game he's ever played. But when the game starts to take over, Chris is forced to face a lean, mean, *medieval* bully.

10656625376